THIS IS THE TEACHER

by **Rhonda Gowler Greene**
illustrated by **Mike Lester**

PUFFIN BOOKS

PUFFIN BOOKS

Published by the Penguin Group

Penguin Young Readers Group, 345 Hudson Street, New York, New York 10014, U.S.A.

Penguin Group (Canada), 90 Eglinton Avenue East, Suite 700, Toronto, Ontario, Canada M4P 2Y3 (a division of Pearson Penguin Canada Inc.)

Penguin Books Ltd, 80 Strand, London WC2R ORL, England

Penguin Ireland, 25 St Stephen's Green, Dublin 2, Ireland (a division of Penguin Books Ltd)

Penguin Group (Australia), 250 Camberwell Road, Camberwell, Victoria 3124, Australia (a division of Pearson Australia Group Pty Ltd)

Penguin Books India Pvt Ltd, 11 Community Centre, Panchsheel Park, New Delhi - 110 017, India

Penguin Group (NZ), Cnr Airborne and Rosedale Roads, Albany, Auckland 1310, New Zealand (a division of Pearson New Zealand Ltd)

Penguin Books (South Africa) (Pty) Ltd, 24 Sturdee Avenue, Rosebank, Johannesburg 2196, South Africa

Registered Offices: Penguin Books Ltd, 80 Strand, London WC2R ORL, England

First published in the United States of America by Dutton Children's Books, a division of Penguin Young Readers Group, 2004
Published by Puffin Books, a division of Penguin Young Readers Group, 2006

10 9 8 7 6 5 4

Text copyright © Rhonda Gowler Greene, 2004
Illustrations copyright © Mike Lester, 2004

Designed by Irene Vandervoort

THE LIBRARY OF CONGRESS HAS CATALOGED THE DUTTON EDITION AS FOLLOWS:

Greene, Rhonda Gowler

This is the teacher / by Rhonda Gowler Greene, illustrated by Mike Lester—1st ed.   p. cm.

Summary: A cumulative rhyme about a teacher's day, from the time the students rush in and drop their lunches, spill the ant farm, and let loose a snake until they file out and head for home.

ISBN: 0-525-47125-1 (hc)

[1. Schools—Fiction. 2. Stories in rhyme. 3. Humorous stories.] 1. Lester, Mike, ill. II. Title.

PZ8.3.G824 Th 2004 [E]—dc21 2002040806

Puffin Books ISBN 0-14-240653-8

Manufactured in China

This is the teacher all ready for school.

These are the students who rush through the door,
who drop sacks of lunches that *smash!* on the floor
and topple the teacher all ready for school.

This is the ant farm that spilled—**oh, my!**—

on top of the desk with the tissue supply

by the students who rushed

and toppled the teacher all ready for school.

This is the snake brought for show-and-tell time
that snuck from its shoe box and slithered and climbed
toward the ants that were spilled
by the students who rushed
and toppled the teacher all ready for school.

This is the girl with the red, runny nose
who shrieked at the ants crawling inside her clothes
and the long snake that climbed
toward the ants that were spilled
by the students who rushed
and toppled the teacher all ready for school.

These are the cupcakes that flew through the air
when the birthday boy slipped and tripped over the chair
of the scared girl who shrieked
at the long snake that climbed
toward the ants that were spilled
by the students who rushed
and toppled the teacher all ready for school.

This is the loose tooth that fell down the drain
and got stuck—*ker-plink!*—so the janitor came

and slid on some cake

by the scared girl who shrieked

at the long snake that climbed

toward the ants that were spilled

by the students who rushed

and toppled the teacher all ready for school.

These are the books that went tumbling—**oops!**—

when passed out in stacks for round reading groups

near the tooth that was found

and the cupcakes that flew

by the scared girl who shrieked

at the long snake that climbed

toward the ants that were spilled

by the students who rushed

and toppled the teacher all ready for school.

THE BEST SCHOOL DAY EVER

THE BEST SCHOOL DAY EVER

THE BEST SCHOOL DAY EVER

This is the hamster that spins in a wheel,

then somehow escapes, making everyone squeal,

and hides by the books

near the tooth that was found

and the cupcakes that flew

by the scared girl who shrieked

at the long snake that climbed

toward the ants that were spilled

by the students who rushed

and toppled the teacher all ready for school.

This is the room
where they gather for lunch,
where their food
spills and *splats!*
as they slurp and they munch.

Eek!

There's that hamster that
spins in a wheel!

This is the ball that was hit with a **whack!**
and soared through the pane with a smashity-**smack!**
near the room where they munched
and— **Eek!** There's that hamster that spins in a wheel!

These are the raindrops that—*plop!*—drizzled down,
soaking their heads and making them frown
after—*whack!*—the ball soared
near the room where they munched
and—**Eek!** There's that hamster that spins in a wheel!

This is the bad bee that buzzed through the crack,
then zoomed round the room in a stinging attack
as the raindrops fell—*plop!*
after—**whack!**—the ball soared
near the room where they munched
and—**Eek!** There's that hamster that spins in a wheel!

This is the fountain that made a huge lake
when its drain was clogged by the show-and-tell snake
as the bad bee went *buzz*
and the raindrops fell—*plop!*
after—*whack!*—the ball soared
near the room where they munched
and—**Eek!** There's that hamster that spins in a wheel!

This is the kid who got sick that day,

so the janitor came with a mop and some spray

by the fountain that clogged

as the bad bee went *buzz*

and the raindrops fell—*plop!*

after—*whack!*—the ball soared

near the room where they munched

and—**Eek!** There's that hamster that spins in a wheel!

This is the mural they made with a *splash!*
and—yikes!—caused the paint cans to teeter and *crash!*
near the kid who got sick
by the fountain that clogged
as the bad bee went *buzz*
and the raindrops fell—*plop!*
after—*whack!*—the ball soared
near the room where they munched
and—**Eek!** There's that hamster that spins in a wheel!

This is the line where they stand, tall and straight,
knowing tomorrow they'll be back by eight
to march by the mural they made with a *splash!*

This is the teacher with books in a bag

who walks from the building, beneath the tall flag,

leading the line

past the mural they made

near the kid who got sick

by the fountain that clogged

as the bad bee went *buzz*

and the raindrops fell—*plop!*

after—*whack!*—the ball soared

near the room where they munched

and that hamster that hid

by the books that fell—*oops!*—

near the tooth that was found

and the cupcakes that flew

by the scared girl who shrieked

at the long snake that climbed

toward the ants that were spilled

by the students who rushed

and toppled the teacher . . .

. . . all ready for bed!